Contents

Chapter 1
The Dare

"Yuck!" I said. The smell was terrible. It made me feel sick. "Something *really* stinks up here!"

"I know," Bebi said with a grin. "Isn't it just the worst thing ever?"

"What is it?" I asked. My eyes were beginning to water.

Bebi smiled at me. "Kenefer," he said, "would you believe it's meant to be medicine?"

"Medicine?" I looked hard at him. "What for?"

"It's my sister's." Bebi pushed the clay dish under my nose, and I jumped back. "The doctor said it would stop her sore tooth hurting."

"More likely to make her throw up," I said. "What's in it?"

Bebi peered at the slimy mess. "I don't know. It looks like mouldy old meat and stinky fat. And chopped up maggots."

Ancient Egyptian Medicine

In fact, Egyptian medicine was rather good. The Egyptians knew a lot about setting bones, and how to treat diseases with herbs. Different doctors treated different diseases. Doctors chanted spells to drive out the evil spirits that had made people ill.

Eye problems were very common (from all the sand blowing about) and so were rotten teeth. The sand got into everything, so most food was full of grit. Teeth were worn down to the gums, and then got infected.

"Ugh!!!" I was trying hard not to look. "Doesn't look much like medicine to me."

"It worked," Bebi said. "My sister took one sniff, and said, 'If you think I'm drinking *that*, think again! I'm *fine!*' Then she got up and went out for a picnic with her friends. The doctor looked very happy. He'd been chanting spells over her for a long time. He said it must have been the spells that cured her."

"If the medicine's worked, why have you kept it?" I asked.

Bebi put the dish down, and looked at me. I didn't like the way he was smiling. Bebi's my best friend. We both like dares, but sometimes he has *gross* ideas.

"I dare you to drink it," he said.

I looked at the stuff Bebi said was medicine.

We were outside on the roof of Bebi's house, and the wind was blowing, but I could still smell it. I could feel my stomach heaving.

And then I had a brilliant idea!

"I know!" I said. "I'll drink half. And I dare *you* to drink the other half!"

Bebi smiled his most evil smile. "OK – but I'll go first!" He pinched his nose, and swallowed half the rotten mess in one huge gulp.

"Delicious," he said, and rubbed his stomach. "Yum yum! Your turn!"

I didn't know what to do. NO WAY was I going to drink that stuff. I picked up the clay dish, and walked to the edge of the roof. I hoped it looked as if I was thinking about the best way to drink it. Then I pointed up at the sky.

"LOOK!" I shouted. Bebi looked up, and I tipped the medicine into the street below.

Maybe I'd have got away with it if only Nefret hadn't been standing in the wrong place. Nefret's a friend of Bebi's sister, and she chose just that moment to come and see her. She was standing outside the door.

Her yell made Bebi's mum come running out. When she saw Nefret – and smelt her – she stormed up the stairs to the roof to find us. I opened my mouth to say it was my fault, but Bebi jumped forward.

"I'm ever so sorry, Mother," he said. "It kind of slipped ..."

His mother put her hands on her hips, and looked at him crossly.

"I had to give the doctor a whole basket of melons for that stuff," she told him. "And Nefret's dress is a real mess. Both of you get down those stairs, and tell her you're sorry. Then you can walk home with her. And after that, you can go down to the river and see if you can find Adib. He promised he'd save a few fish for me."

"Great!" Bebi said. "It's been nothing but boring old bread and onions for supper for weeks!"

"That," said his mother, "is total and utter rubbish, and you know it. Now – off with you! And hurry back! I don't want the fish to smell the house out too!"

Chapter 2
Nefret Gets Her Own Back

When we got down the stairs, Nefret was waiting, and she was mad! She's older than me and Bebi, and she's evil. She glared at us as we came out onto the dusty road.

"You two are going to pay for this," she said. "BIG time!"

"I'm really sorry," I said. "It was me that threw the stuff. I never thought to look."

"No – it was MY fault," Bebi said. "It was me that dared Kenefer."

"You dared him to do *what*?" Nefret asked. "Throw that muck over my clothes?"

Bebi shook his head. "No. I dared him to drink it. It's my sister's medicine."

"MEDICINE?" Nefret looked horrified. "What kind of a doctor do you go to? What's it for?"

"Toothache," Bebi said.

"That's crazy," Nefret told him. "Everyone knows you should chew willow for toothache." She turned to me. "So why did you throw that horrible stuff all over my dress?"

"I didn't mean to," I said. "I promise. I was trying to make Bebi think I'd drunk it."

"Well," Nefret said, and her eyes were gleaming. "If you two like dares so much, I'll give you one. A taste of your own medicine, you might say."

Bebi and I didn't say anything.

"I dare you to go to the Place of Purification," Nefret said. "I dare you to find old Seneb's tent, and go right inside."

The Place of Purification

This was the place where dead bodies had their internal organs taken out. That's your liver, guts, lungs and stomach. Then the bodies were dried out. The Egyptians thought this would make the bodies pure, and ready for the next stage.

After that they said special spells over them, and wrapped the bodies up in bandages. This is mummification, or making the bodies into mummies.

> Different people did different jobs. If you were the person who took out the internal organs, you didn't wrap up the bodies.
>
> The Egyptians called the Place of Purification "Ibu."

Nefret giggled. "There'll be some good smells in there! And you can bring me something back, so I know you've really and truly been there. Bring me back a charm. One of the charms for the dead! Oh, and if you don't ..."

Nefret thought for a moment.

"If you don't go," she went on, "I'll tell my sisters you spoiled my dress on purpose! They won't let you get away with that!" And then she ran away down the street, laughing loudly.

Bebi and I looked at each other. Nefret's sisters were big. And strong. All three of them were training to be acrobats. They were well known for being tough.

"We'll have to do it," I said. "We can't be beaten up by a gang of girls! Everyone would hear about it."

It was true. Everyone always knows everything in our village.

Bebi nodded. "Tell you what – let's go now. Get it over with. We'll get the fish on the way back."

Chapter 3
Be Careful Where You Walk ...

It was a long walk to the Place of Purification. It's beyond the village, on the river bank. I'd never been that way before. I knew what happened there, of course. It's where the dead people are made ready for their journey to the after life ... the Field of Reeds is what my mother calls it. My grandmother calls it the Wonderful Land. She says she can't wait to get there, because she'll see my grandfather again.

Also, she won't have to hear my sisters screeching at each other. I don't know what my father calls it. He's been away with the army for so long I can hardly remember what he looks like.

Anyway, Bebi and I walked and ran through the narrow streets. We took care to jump over the rubbish.

I don't know what your village is like, but in ours a lot of the houses are close together. Some of them are tall, too – up to three floors high. The shadows are dark, even in the middle of the day.

You always have to watch where you're walking. My mother and Bebi's mother take care where they chuck their rubbish, but not everyone does. If you leave your rubbish in the shadows it takes much longer to dry out, because the sun can't reach it.

And, of course, it's not just melon skins and fish bones and lettuce leaves I'm talking about.

You can guess what I mean.

Human waste!

It must be wonderful to be rich. Then you'd have a special room for that kind of thing – and a servant to empty it away! We have to take ours into the fields behind the houses, and I hate it when it's my turn.

Bebi suddenly grabbed my arm, and pulled me into a doorway. We were only just in time. A torrent of filthy water poured down almost on top of us.

"Watch out!" Bebi yelled. A woman peered down from a roof high above.

"Sorry, boys," she said, and laughed. "Here! Catch!"

I couldn't see anything when I looked up. The sky was too bright. But Bebi stepped forward. He held out his hands ... and a fig dropped into them.

"Wow!" he said. "Thank you!"

The woman laughed again, and vanished.

"She must be *really* rich," Bebi said. "Fancy having all that water to chuck away!"

I was picking bits of soggy barley bread off my feet. "I don't think it's water," I said. "I think it's beer. Beer that's been kept too long. Phew! What a waste!"

Bebi slapped me on the back. "We're not having a good day, are we? Hey – do you want the fig?"

I stared at him. We always shared things. Our rule was half each. One of us cut, the other chose.

"Don't you feel well?" I asked.

"I'm fine," Bebi said, but even when I pulled the fig in half he still said he didn't want any.

That was OK by me. I ate it all, and it was great. It almost made me forget we were on our way to old Seneb's tent ... and a very nasty dare. Almost.

Chapter 4
Seneb – Cheap and MEAN!

Maybe I should tell you about Seneb. He's well known in our town – in the wrong sort of way.

His family have always been embalmers just like my family are all soldiers.

Embalmers

Embalmers were the people who looked after the bodies of the dead, and dried them out ready for the next stage. An embalmed body was dry, and wouldn't rot or decay.

You could choose between a top rate (and expensive) embalmer ...

...or someone like Seneb, who was much cheaper.

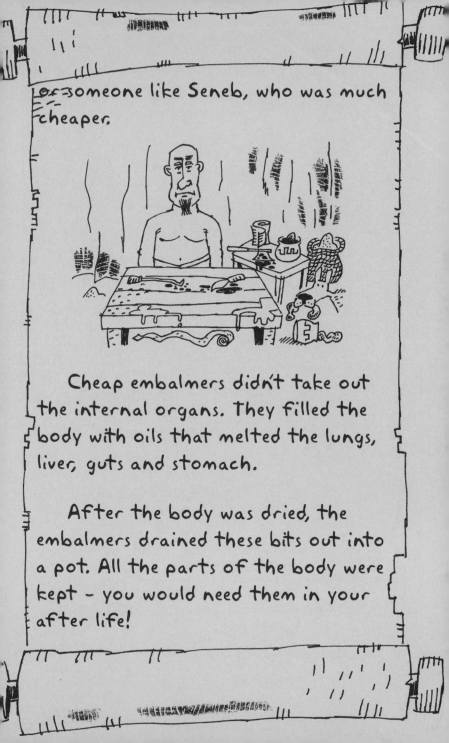

Cheap embalmers didn't take out the internal organs. They filled the body with oils that melted the lungs, liver, guts and stomach.

After the body was dried, the embalmers drained these bits out into a pot. All the parts of the body were kept - you would need them in your after life!

I'll be a soldier too, one day, like my father. Bebi will be a farmer, like his father. And one day Nefret will be an acrobat like her sisters. That's a scary thought. Knowing her, she'll throw crocodiles to her sisters for laughs!

Crocodiles

The Egyptians thought crocodiles were sacred and holy. They belonged to Sobek, the god of the Nile waters. Rich Egyptians often kept crocodiles in their pools to bring fortune from the gods. When they drew Sobek, he was sometimes a crocodile, or sometimes a man with a crocodile head.

Anyway, Seneb had a problem. A BIG
problem ... his wife. She wanted Seneb to be
the most important embalmer ever. She
made his life miserable. She told him he
was wasting his time in our village. She
told him he should go somewhere better.
She told him he must go away and seek his
fortune. She told him not to come back
until he was rich. She ordered Seneb to go
down the Nile to the Valley of the Kings ...
and he did. He was fed up with the nagging.
He borrowed a boat, and off he went.

The Valley of the Kings

The Valley of the Kings was where the pharoahs, or kings, of the New Kingdom of Egypt (1500BC - 1100BC) were buried.

Tutankhamun - who's famous now - was buried there. The kings were buried in the Valley to try and stop the grave robbers.

The kings were buried with so much gold, and so many costly things (to use in the after life), that robbers were always trying to break in.

Many of the tombs of the early pharaohs had been broken into and destroyed. So in the Valley of the Kings, they dug tombs out of solid stone. But the thieves still found a way to get into them.

When Seneb got to the Valley of the Kings, he was amazed at what he saw. Hundreds of people work there. They tidy up the old tombs and burial chambers, and prepare them for new burials.

My mother says that in the old days only kings and nobles and rich people were embalmed in the proper way. A lot of trouble was taken to prepare them for the great journey to the after life. More people can afford it now ... like our family. It would have been awful if my grandfather hadn't had a proper coffin. A scribe wrote descriptions of all his good deeds on it. My mother said it cost a lot, but it was worth it.

Anyway, Seneb went to the Valley of the Kings. He found the priests in charge, and told them he was Seneb, Master Embalmer. He said he was so well known that families would come to him and beg him on bended knees to look after their loved ones. He told *so* many lies!

I wouldn't mind betting he never gets to the Heavenly Fields. When the gods put his heart on the weighing scales, it'll go *doink!!!* and they'll tell him he's failed the test. That old crocodile god Ammut (may she be praised and live for ever) will be chomping him up for certain.

Ammut

Ammut was more of a demon than a god. Kenefer is being extra polite to say she's a crocodile god. It was always a good thing to be polite about demons in case they remembered you'd been rude after you'd died.

The Egyptians believed that after you died, your heart was put on some scales and weighed against a feather.

That would show if you'd been good or bad in your life. If your heart was heavy with wicked deeds, Ammut would eat it up, and you would never reach the after life. Ammut had the head of a crocodile, the body of a lion, and the back legs of a hippo!

It might seem odd, but one of the priests believed Seneb. He told him he could prepare the body of a man who had just died. Seneb was thrilled, and at first it was fine.

It all went wrong when the other embalmers heard about Seneb. They worked in the Valley of the Kings. They lived near the valley and they did NOT want anyone new taking their work. They wouldn't work with Seneb. They hid his tools. They broke his pots of palm wine. (That's what the bodies are washed with. My mother told me.) They wouldn't tell Seneb where to find the perfumed oils he needed ... and in the end he got the message.

Seneb left in the middle of the night and came back to our village. He was *so* angry! He was angry with the embalmers from the Valley of the Kings and he was angry with his wife. My mother said he swore he'd never ever talk to a woman again. He made his wife so miserable, she divorced him ... but I think it was just as much her fault as his.

Seneb's been angry ever since, and it's not just with women. He glowers and mutters and growls at everyone.

And that's why I was feeling very wobbly. I didn't want to go to the Place of Purification. I was scared of Seneb. Really scared!

Chapter 5

Horrible Smells and Buzzing Flies

As we got nearer the Place of Purification we both slowed down. We were away from the houses, and walking on the hard mud track that runs beside the river. On one side of us were reeds and rough grass and water, and on the other a date palm orchard. For once we weren't thinking about helping ourselves to the dates.

Beyond the orchard was a flat sandy area ... and that's where we were heading.

There are always smells of rotting food and stuff in the streets at home. You get used to it. I don't think I'd ever get used to the smell that was beginning to hover round us that afternoon. It was worse than the medicine. Much, much worse. And there were SO many flies. They clustered round us, and however much we batted them away, they kept coming back.

Bebi began to cough, and I saw he was very pale. He saw me looking at him, and made a face.

"Do you remember when we found that dead cow?" he asked.

I wished I didn't, but I did.

"Well – do you think dead human bodies are like that? All maggotty?"

"Of course they aren't," I said. "They get really well looked after. They couldn't enjoy themselves in the afterlife if they were maggotty."

Bebi didn't look as if he believed me. He said, "What about people like Edfu? You know. That carpenter – the one that stole a pig."

"What do you mean?" I asked.

"Well – he had his ears chopped off, didn't he?"

I rubbed my own ears to make sure they were still there. "Yes. So what?"

"So will he have no ears for ever and ever?" Bebi was frowning.

"I don't know," I said. "Maybe he'll get them back. Maybe the embalmers could make him false ears. Grandmother said they made my grandfather new fingers."

Bebi stopped and stared at me. "New fingers? Why? Was he a thief? Did he have them cut off?"

"Of course not," I said. "He was a soldier! He lost them in a battle."

"Oh," Bebi said. "Sorry. I didn't know."

Punishments

Most people were beaten as their punishment if they did wrong. But it depended on where you lived, and who was in charge. The pharaoh, or king, had hundreds of different sorts of officers who were in charge of law and order. Some were more harsh than others.

There were law courts where people could bring complaints - "Someone has stolen my ox!" And that's where people were judged if they had been found doing wrong.

The police officers looked for clues, and sometimes used dogs to sniff people out.

You could have your ears cut off,
or other body parts, to make you
confess to something they thought
you'd done. If it then turned out you
were innocent, it was just hard luck!

When you died, you could have false
ears made, so you would be complete
again in the after life.

I had to force myself to keep walking
towards the tents. They were open on two
sides so the wind could blow through, and
we were near enough now to see men
moving about inside. Bebi kept gulping. I
knew he didn't want to go any nearer, and
neither did I. We couldn't go back, though. A
dare is a dare.

Chapter 6
Got You!

Seneb's tent was smaller than the others. It was the nearest too. That was lucky for us – or maybe, unlucky. I was glad to see that Seneb had his back to us. He was bent over a low wooden table, and I thought I saw the flash of a knife.

I couldn't see exactly what was lying on the table. I didn't want to see, either. Then Seneb picked up a basket full of something that looked like natron. I'd seen lots of it before. It looks a bit like salt. My mother uses it for cleaning fat and grease off our clothes.

Natron

Kenefer's mother used natron to soak up fat and grease. The embalmers used it to dry out the fats and fluids in bodies.

Seneb tipped the natron over the thing on the table. I knew now that the thing was a dead body. Ugh. Then he picked up another basket. More natron. When he'd tipped that out, he looked round. He must have thought there was still another basket.

There wasn't.

We heard him swear loudly. Then he
scooped up the empty baskets, and marched
out of the tent.

"*Now!*" Bebi hissed in my ear. "Quick!
We can be in that tent and out again before
he gets back!"

I didn't stop to think. If I had, I'd never have moved. I took a deep breath, held my nose, and ran ... and there we were. Inside the tent. There were bowls and pots all around us. The stench was so strong you could almost *see* it. The table was right in front of us, heaped high with natron ... but it didn't quite cover everything.

Sticking out at one end were legs. Thin, skinny legs.

Three legs.

We turned to run – but I hadn't seen the row of pottery jars. I tripped over the biggest, and crashed onto the hard earth. As I struggled to my feet I heard Bebi hiss, "Quick! He's coming back! Run!" And he was off like a rabbit.

I was half way through the tent flap when a heavy hand grabbed my arm.

"*Gotcha!*" said a voice.

Seneb's voice.

I tried to wriggle free, but it was no good. He had my arm in a tight grip.

"Little kids aren't welcome here," he growled. "Sneaking around a sacred place! I've a good mind to take you to the priest. Don't you know it's forbidden for dirty little boys to come anywhere near these tents?"

I nodded.

"Then why are you here?" And he shook me until my teeth rattled.

"I'm – very – very – sorry!" I said as soon as I could speak. "It was a dare!"

Seneb shook me again. "*A dare*? You nasty little worm! Creeping in to spy, more like. Want to know what goes on here, do you? Heard all the stories, have you? You'll be grateful for people like me when you're dead, you little snoop!"

I made a sort of gasping noise. It was all I could manage.

"Right! If you want to know what I'm doing, I'll tell you!" Seneb dumped me back onto my feet, but he kept a firm grip on my arm. "Are you listening?"

He didn't wait for my answer. He was smiling – but it wasn't a nice smile. "In fact, little worm, I'll tell you what I'd do if YOU were served up here!"

I didn't feel good. I didn't feel good at all. But there wasn't anything I could do. Seneb's face was so close to mine I could see the hairs in his nose. And his rotten teeth. His breath was hot on my cheek.

"Do you see that knife?" He pointed to a nasty-looking curved blade. "That's a slitting knife. Opens up the body. And you see those four jars? If you were lucky – very lucky – we'd put your liver, and your lungs in those. And your stomach and your guts."

He snorted. I think it was meant to be a laugh. "Only you'd never be that lucky. Little nothings like you don't get that sort of treatment. That's only for the rich. For the important people. Little nothings like you – you get nothing." He snorted again. "You'd be like my friend over there on the table. We'd wash out your guts and then dry you out. No packing or stuffing or painting for you. 40 days under the natron, and you'd be ready. And a whole cartload less trouble than you are today! Now – any questions?"

Canopic jars

These four jars were where the embalmers put the liver, the lungs, the stomach and the guts when they were dealing with a rich person's burial. The jars were buried with the mummy. So was anything else that had been used.

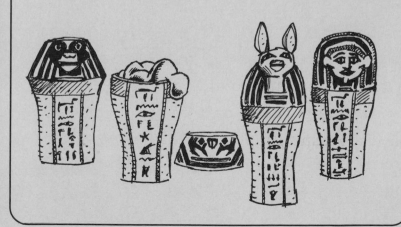

The Egyptians thought the heart was the most important organ. That was left inside the body - for the gods to weigh. Brains weren't important at all. Sometimes they were pulled out of the skull by a metal hook pushed up one nostril, and sometimes they were melted and flushed out with special oils.

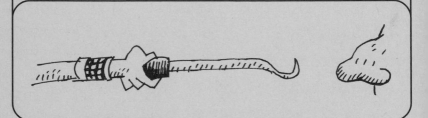

I couldn't say anything. I hadn't really heard much of what Seneb had been saying. All I could think about was the Thing on the table. I tried to look at Seneb's nose. I tried to count the hundreds of flies buzzing round his head. I tried to work out the chances of Bebi waiting for me.

None of it worked. I couldn't stop staring at those three long stiff skinny legs, and the three skinny feet. Even when Seneb's big face got in the way I could see them in my head. I couldn't think of anything else. What WAS it?

Seneb's nose was an inch in front of mine. *"You're not listening, little worm!"* he bellowed. *"I said, any questions?"*

"Yes," I said. "Why has that man got three legs?"

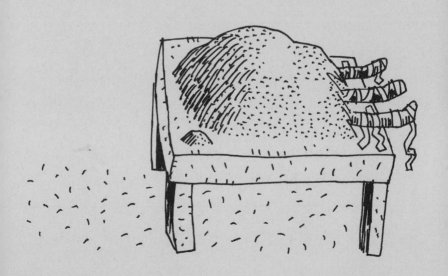

Chapter 7
The Blue Scarab

For a moment I thought Seneb was going to strangle me. And then I thought he'd gone mad. He threw his head back, and he laughed and laughed until spit dribbled down his chin. He wiped his hand across his face, and then laughed some more.

I stood and stared at him. Part of me was saying, "Run! You can get away now!" but the other part wanted to know. I knew

I'd have nightmares for ever if I didn't find out.

WHY did the man have three legs?

There was the sudden sound of voices outside, and two burly men pushed their way into the tent. They were dressed the same way as Seneb, so I guessed they were embalmers as well. They looked amazed when they saw me.

"What are *you* doing here, boy?" one asked. "Don't you know this is a sacred place?"

"Yes," I said. "I'm very sorry."

The other man was staring at me. "Was it you who made Seneb laugh?" he asked.

I shuffled my feet. "Erm ... I don't know," I muttered.

"If you did," he said, "that's a miracle. He's the gloomiest man in all Egypt – isn't that right, Seneb?"

I blinked. Seneb, amazingly, was still grinning. "This sprat – he thinks I've got a three-legged man in here!" he spluttered. And off he went again, howling with laughter.

The man who had spoken first put his hand into a pottery bowl, and slowly pulled out a large blue scarab – a magic charm. He handed it to me.

"Young man," he said, "we've been trying to make Seneb laugh for years – and we never could. Keep this scarab for yourself because you've done what all of us grown men couldn't do. And now – hop it, before we call the priest!"

Scarabs

A scarab was one of the magic charms to protect the body. The embalmers wrapped them in between the bands of linen cloth, with other charms. All the time the body was being wrapped, a priest was saying prayers to make the magic work better to protect the body and send it safely to the after life.

"Yes," I said. "Thank you ... " I didn't move.

The man folded his arms and glared at me. "Didn't you hear what I said?"

Seneb, his eyes still streaming, pushed his way forward. "He wants to know about the three legs," he said, and he slapped me so hard on the back I nearly fell over. "I'll tell you, boy – it's a *dog*! A great big dog – Lord Seth's dog."

I couldn't understand what he was saying. "But dogs have four legs ..." I began.

"Not this dog – it lost a leg to a crocodile years back when they were hunting." Seneb was grinning with all his rotten teeth showing. "They called him Trio. I'll pack a fourth leg for him when I wrap him up ..." He began to rock with laughter again. "And you thought it was a man! That'll teach you to come spying!"

Animals

Animals were very often embalmed and made into mummies. Even fish mummies have been found, and thousands and **THOUSANDS** of cats! The Egyptians loved their pets.

I tucked the scarab into my cloth belt, slipped out of the tent, and ran. I ran like the wind, and half way back to the orchard I found Bebi running beside me.

"Are you OK?" he panted.

"Yeah – " I said, and I was too much out of breath to say anything else until we flung ourselves down under a tree.

"Thanks for staying," I said when I'd got my breath back. I was being sarcastic.

Bebi looked very embarrassed. "I'm sorry," he said. Then he gave me an odd sideways look. "If you want to know – I had to rush off and be sick."

"Sick?" I said.

He nodded. "It must have been the medicine. You were quite right to chuck it away."

"Oh! Right!" I suddenly began to feel really happy. Bebi had never ever said he was sorry to me before.

"So," he said, "shall we go and get my mum's fish? If we go the long way round we won't bump into Nefret."

I felt in my cloth belt, and smiled to myself. "Why worry about her?" I said.

"You know what she's like," Bebi went on. "She's sure to be waiting for us so she can have a go at us for not getting anything from Seneb's tent."

I stood up, and held out the scarab on the palm of my hand.

Bebi stared. "Wow!" he said. "Wow! How on earth did you get that without Seneb seeing you?"

I gave a shrug as if it didn't matter much, as if it had been dead easy. "I'll tell you on the way to the market," I said.

"It was all because of this three-legged mummy …"

AUTHOR FACT FILE
VIVIAN FRENCH

What makes you feel like you're going to be sick?
Slugs – most of all if they've been squished!

Would you like to have lived in Ancient Egypt?
Why or why not?
**I'd have loved to live in Ancient Egypt. They had
a great way of life, and there was a lot of music
and dancing and having fun!**

What's the worst punishment you've ever received?
**Erm ... I think it was when I had to write
hundreds of lines when I was at school. It was
so BORING!!!**

What's the most disgusting thing you've ever eaten?
**Half a caterpillar in a lettuce. The other end
was still wriggling about when I found out!**

ILLUSTRATOR FACT FILE
DAVE SUTTON

What makes you feel like you're going to be sick?
Bugs in my food. Even the IDEA of bugs in my food.

Would you like to have lived in Ancient Egypt? Why or why not?
Yes, it looks like there was a lot of fun to be had. It wasn't all slaves and serving rich people.

What's the worst punishment you've ever received?
At school, I was given the ruler across my butt for drawing pictures on my desk.

What's the most disgusting thing you've ever eaten?
On holiday I got given some soup with a maggot-looking thing sitting on top. I thought it was a fancy topping, so I took a little nibble but left most of it. When the waiter came to take away the plates I asked what the topping had been. He looked at it, went "yuk", then showed it to the other staff – all of whom went "yuk" too!

Barrington Stoke would like to thank all its readers for commenting on the manuscript before publication and in particular:

Adam Birch	Felicity Juckes
Jonathan Brough	Lottie MacDonald
Mackenzie Dearsley	Harriet Mallender
Cordelia Drew	Stephanie Poulengeris
Yasmin Duffy	Jack Lacey
Olivia Frame	Gilbert Ratcliffe
Kristina Goncharov	

Become a Consultant!

Would you like to give us feedback on our titles before they are published? Contact us at the email address below – we'd love to hear from you!

info@barringtonstoke.co.uk
www.barringtonstoke.co.uk

Try another book in the "fyi" series!
Fiction with stacks of facts

Boxing
The Greatest by Alan Gibbons

Rock Music
Diary of a Trainee Rock God
by Jonathan Meres

Scottish History and Literature
Dead Man's Close by Catherine MacPhail

All available from our website:
www.barringtonstoke.co.uk